DR. COO and the PIGEON PROTEST

Sarah Hampson 🍃 Kass Reich

KIDS CAN PRESS

Dr. Archibald Coo was a big-city kind of pigeon.
He was sophisticated.
He knew how to get around.
He knew how to land in just the right places.

He had favorite perches
in the city ...

The edges of beautiful buildings.
(He was friends with gargoyles.)

Statues.
(Heads were better
than shoulders.)

Park benches that offered a view.

It's true that Dr. Coo would often look down his beak in a way that made him seem very serious. But he wasn't always. It's just that, deep in his feathers, he was a curious sort. He observed the way of the world as he flew about it.

Dr. Coo knew things.

And he knew he had a problem. Or rather, he could see that there was a problem with pigeons.

One day, Dr. Coo was perched with his pigeon pals on a wire.

There was Hootie Claw. He was a young pigeon with recently acquired flying feathers.

Alongside Hootie perched Vern Birdman, a shy fellow in a light-brown suit. In the pecking order, he was happy to be last.

And then in flew Dove Blanchett. She prided herself on her shiny coat, which she kept spotlessly clean. "I'm part turtledove," she liked to tweet with her beak in the air.

The conversation started out as it normally did.
They cackled about the supply of corn kernels
in the park.
They nattered about the nearing of winter.
They prattled about new perches.

But then, Hootie Claw dared to bring up something they all had been thinking for a very long time.

"We pigeons get no respect!" he blurted.

"Those humans down there" — Hootie pecked at the air to indicate the people below on the streets — "they hate us. They shoo us away!"

"There, there," cooed Vern, hopping a little closer to Hootie and nudging him with his wing. "Calm down."

"Calm down?" hooted Hootie. "No one appreciates us! I'm the voice of the next-generation pigeon, and I'm not standing for it!"

Oh, yes, he was in a flap.

"I know what Hootie means," offered Dove softly. "When people see a bluebird, they sigh and get dreamy-eyed. They call them 'little fellows.'

"If they hear a cardinal sing ... well, that's even worse! You'd think they'd never heard a bird before.

"And it's the same with robins. They can't wait for them to arrive!

"But we're just as beautiful!" She shook raindrops from her glossy coat and held her little head up high.

Vern twitched a bit, uncertain if he should say anything.

But then, he thought about the time a car almost ran him down — on purpose.

He recalled the lady who swung her umbrella at him — for no reason!

"Some people say we're rats with wings," he observed with a gentle sigh.

At this point, Hootie, Dove and Vern looked down the line to Dr. Coo.

"It's the way of the modern world," cooed Dr. Coo. "It used to be different."

As the pigeons leaned in, blinking with curiosity, Dr. Coo told them of the dreams he often had, while he nestled with the gargoyles high up in the sky.

"Pigeons were once like angels," he said wistfully, summoning his visions of another time.

"They accompanied the gods in ancient worlds.

"They delivered news of the Olympic Games in ancient Greece.

"They were revered as signs of peace and love and wisdom and beauty."

"I have seen pigeons in important wars,"
Dr. Coo continued dreamily, "fearlessly flying into
danger with notes strapped to their backs.

"They delivered messages to soldiers in battle.

"They carried medicine across battlefields strewn
with injured men.

"They were heroes!"

"I knew it!" cried Hootie, hopping up and down on the wire. "I knew we were special!"

Timidly, Vern piped up again. "What should we do, Dr. Coo?"

"We need a plan!" cried Hootie.

"We need to be loved again!" Dove sang.

Dr. Coo turned his head one way. And then the other.

He hummed. He hooted. He pecked. And he pondered.

Then he coo-cooed his plan into the ears of his companions — and off they flew to spread the word to other pigeons in the city.

The next morning, all the pigeons had disappeared!
The squares were empty.
So were park benches.
On the edges of buildings, the gargoyles were lonely.
It was eerie.
The people in the city were the ones who were
nattering now.
"What does this mean?" they whispered worriedly
to one another.

Those who came to the parks with bread crumbs and corn kernels were sad.

They spread out their offerings on the pavement.

They reached out their arms in friendship.

But still, no pigeons came.

Nothing felt the same.

The pigeons had been part of the life of the big, busy city.

Part of what filled the sky with mystery.

With beauty.

Part of what made the parks come alive.

Soon, people asked the mayor what to do.

But she had no clue.

That was when Dr. Archibald Coo flew to the ledge outside the mayor's office. He clutched a small book about the history of the pigeon, and on his little leg was strapped a letter.

Dear Ms. Mayor,

We pigeons have flown the coop because we feel unwelcome in our own home. A city is a place for all kinds. We love it here. Pigeons and people must learn to get along.

We will refrain from splatting on cars (and heads!). Let's create composting areas in parks for our droppings. This will keep statues and public spaces clean — and create rich fertilizer for our city's green spaces.

In return, we ask that you remove the spikes that keep us off ledges. Don't shoo us away — be neighborly. Stop and say hello! And, please, no more running us down with your cars.

Let's remember the history of cooperation between people and pigeons and enjoy living together in our beautiful city.

Yours, in feathers and stripes,

Dr. Archibald Coo

The mayor was moved to a tear or two. She shook Dr. Coo's claw.

That summer, the city held the first annual Pigeon Parade to celebrate diversity and friendship. At an appointed time, a flock of pigeons filled the sky, like sudden laughter in a room.

When the pigeons were over the crowds, they released something surprising. Not the usual droppings people had come to expect. But little notes untied from the straps on their legs.

The notes gently fluttered down, landing on people's heads, on their shoulders, on their cars. And everyone eagerly caught them.

For Henry Bernard Clarridge, my first grandchild — S.H.

To my sisters Steph and Kate, who appreciate all animals
from the city to the seaside — K.S.

Text © 2018 Sarah Hampson

Illustrations © 2018 Kass Reich

Kids Can Press gratefully acknowledges the financial support of the Government
of Ontario, through the Ontario Media Development Corporation; the Ontario
Arts Council; the Canada Council for the Arts; and the Government of Canada,
through the CBF, for our publishing activity.

Published in Canada and the U.S. by Kids Can Press Ltd.
25 Dockside Drive, Toronto, ON M5A 0B5

Kids Can Press is a Corus Entertainment Inc. Company

www.kidscanpress.com

The artwork in this book was rendered with gouache paint
and colored pencils, with final touches added digitally.
The text is set in Bembo.

Edited by Jennifer Stokes
Designed by Julia Naimska

Printed and bound in Malaysia, in 9/2017 by Tien Wah Press (Pte.) Ltd.

CM 18 0 9 8 7 6 5 4 3 2 1

Library and Archives Canada Cataloguing in Publication

Hampson, Sarah, author

    Dr. Coo and the pigeon protest / written by
Sarah Hampson ; illustrated by Kass Reich.

ISBN 978-1-77138-361-5 (hardcover)

    I. Reich, Kass, illustrator II. Title.

PS8615.A5455D72 2018   jC813'.6   C2017-902759-X